DATE			

The Sand Castle

Other books by Rita Mae Brown:

The Sand Castle

Rita Mae Brown

Grove Press
New York

First published in the German language in 2007 by Mare Buchverlag, Hamburg, Germany

Printed in the United States of America
Published simultaneously in Canada

ISBN-10: 0-8021-1870-4
iSBN-13: 978-0-8021-1870-7

Grove Press
an imprint of Grove/Atlantic, Inc.
841 Broadway
New York, NY 10003

Distributed by Publishers Group West

www.groveatlantic.com

08 09 10 11 12   10 9 8 7 6 5 4 3 2

Fic.

Semper Fi
In Memory of
Uncle Ken

The Sand Castle

A white-hinged sign with a big red crab painted on it loomed out of the thinning fog.

"Jesus." Mother swerved to the right.

Her sister, Louise, replied sharply, "Thou shalt not take the name of the Lord in vain."

"I didn't, you twit, I took his son's."

"The Holy Trinity, Father, Son, and Holy Ghost. Same."

"This is supposed to be a trip to the Bay. If I want religious instruction I'll go to church."

"Well, that's just it, isn't it?" Louise was smug. "You're a Lutheran, which is God's punishment. Otherwise you'd worship at the One True Church."

Mother, sidestepping the bait for a fight dangled by her older sister—just how much older also a ripe subject for contention—shrugged. "God will forgive me, that's His trade."

Louise, pretty in what she deemed her mid-forties, crossed her arms over her chest. She was closer to fifty-two or fifty-three.

Awakened by the swerve, I piped up, "How long till we get there?"

"Not long." Mother avoided being specific.

"Forty-five minutes. If this fog would lift we'd get there faster." Louise feared driving in fog, which was sensible.

Mother feared nothing. At least that's what I thought at seven. Although Mother drove, we rumbled along in Aunt Wheezie's new black Nash with the dull gray interior. I hated the car but kept that opinion to myself. Why would anyone want to drive a car that looked like a cockroach? Even at seven I was a gearhead, which delighted my father and amused my mother.

Leroy, still asleep next to me, evidenced no interest in motors even though he was a boy. He'd turned eight in June. I wouldn't reach that advanced age until November, so those extra months pleased him even if cars did not.

"I love the Chesapeake Bay." Mother smiled as the first sliver of pink appeared on the horizon, the fog thinning in places. "Wheeze, remember when Aunt Doney and Uncle Jim took us down here for the Fourth of July? I must have been Nickel's age."

Louise smiled broadly, "Aunt Doney wore so much linen and gauze she looked like an Arab."

"She was so fair," Mother remarked.

"I'll never forget when you and I got tan and she had a hissy. Said we looked like field hands."

"Better field hands than cadavers." Mother felt like someone had told her what to do and how to do it every step of her life and Aunt Doney was no exception.

"She had a point, I guess, but we were in our teens then and Coco Chanel started the fad for white clothes in summer, and a tan. Oh, remember that French boater striped top I wore? Blue and white. I just thought that was the most beautiful thing."

"It was."

"And that's why I never let you borrow it. You'd have torn it or spilled something on it. Juts, you're so rough sometimes. Just watching you dance is exhausting."

"Mother, when were you and Aunt Wheezie here with Aunt Doney and Uncle Jim?"

"I think the first time was 1912. Took forever to get here. There used to be a spur line so you could take the train to St. Mary's. We stayed a whole week."

Aunt Louise, to remind me of what I already knew—because I really liked history—said, "A few rich people owned cars as toys. You took

4

a trolley, a train, or a horse-drawn buggy. Didn't Mrs. Chalfonte get the first car in Runnymede?"

"No, her brother did. The brother was killed in the war," Mother replied.

"Same war as PopPop?" I asked.

"Same war," Aunt Louise affirmed. "I pray to God there will never be another one. It was the war to end all wars."

"We know better." Mother slowed for an S curve. A truck with wooden panels on the sides to hold in its load of hay was lurching toward us from the opposite direction.

"World War Two is still World War One." Aunt Louise stared out the window, the lifting fog now bright pink.

"Why?"

"Didn't settle the issues the first time." Aunt Louise, not a keen student of history, paid attention to current affairs and for her these had been current.

"War will always be with us. People like to kill each other," Mother stated flatly.

"If the peoples of the world accept Christ, war would end forever."

"Aunt Wheezie, how can they accept Christ if they have their own God?"

"They're wrong." This was said with finality and conviction.

"Oh." I didn't press it mostly because religion fascinated me much less than horses, cars, and history.

"Let's go back to that place for lunch," Mother suggested.

"It's forty-five minutes from St. Mary's." Aunt Louise named the county at the southern tip of southern Maryland. The little town there was called St. Mary's City.

"You're right. Okay, Nick, you keep your eyes peeled for another sign like that and we'll stop for lunch on the way home. We can't stay here all day, which is why we started so early. Anyway, I love to see the Bay when the sun comes up and the birds are flying around and talking to one another. And you know it's August and the coots will be flying in for a rest."

Coots were a type of duck that migrated. In wintertime other types of ducks stayed on the Bay, over a million of them.

"Juts, birds don't talk to one another." Louise shook her head at her fanciful younger sister.

"They do. We don't understand it, that's all." She breathed in, quickly changing the subject because Louise could be contrary and she was edging on it today. "Think Aunt Doney could make the trip?"

"To St. Mary's County?"

"Well, yes. We could fix up the back seat and she could sleep. There are folding wheelchairs."

"No matter. They won't push in the sand."

Mother sighed. "You're right."

These words, more than any other, guaranteed happiness for Louise.

"How old is Aunt Doney?" I asked.

"Ninety-eight," Louise replied.

"Oh." I couldn't fathom this but I did know that the maternal side of our family routinely lived a long time. We had Bibles going back to 1620 and written in various beautiful hands were the birthdays and death days of our forebearers. A lot of the men died in wars but those women who survived childhood seemed semi-immortal. As it was, Aunt Doney's brother was still alive and he'd fought in the War Between the States, being not much older than myself at the time. He was in a wheelchair, too. It made me wonder if you could live too long.

Mother checked the rearview mirror. "That boy can sleep through a thunderstorm."

"He sleeps a lot since Ginny died." Louise's voice lowered.

Ginny, her daughter, had died in February 1952, six months back, at age thirty-three. Leroy cried a lot. Everyone did, including

Leroy's father, a marine with the Sixth Division, who had been a war hero at Okinawa. That shocked me, and scared me, too.

"Children are made of rubber. He'll bounce back." Mother kept a positive outlook.

"I don't know, Juts. I hope so. It takes a lot of living to understand death. He's eight. Imagine if we'd lost Momma at eight."

"We would have had each other." Mother stopped herself from making light of it. "But I expect we would have cried ourselves to sleep for a long, long time."

"And the poor little guy has to live up to Ken. How can he do that? How do you live up to a father who won the Distinguished Service Medal for conspicuous bravery?"

"Sis, Leroy isn't the first one of our family to have a hero father. One of us has been in every war or uprising since the Jamestown Massacre. If they managed, so can he."

The Jamestown Massacre occurred in 1622,

on Good Friday, along the James River in Virginia.

"That's Chessy's family not ours. Never forget, Julia," she used Mother's full name, "We're Marylanders."

"Still. There's always been someone in a war somewhere. There will always be war." She cut off Louise's protest. "You know yourself that Americans don't all follow the word so why would you think someone in the Ukraine will? It's just the way it is."

"Makes me sick." Louise meant it.

"I guess it would make me sick if I had to see it and smell it." Mother glanced to the left, the east. We were nearing the point of St. Mary's County and the sun was breaking over where the Chesapeake Bay meets the Potomac River at Point Lookout. Virginia reposed to the west and the other chunk of Maryland to the east. Islands had broken off eastern Maryland and sat in the Bay like pieces of a jigsaw puzzle.

"You tickle me." Louise smiled.

"Why?"

"You'd clap your hands when the sun came up when you were little. Momma would laugh and you'd clap more." She sighed.

"What's better than a new day?" Mother beamed.

Their mother, Cora, died in 1947. I was almost three. I remembered everyone crying. That was my first brush with someone leaving Earth. Next came one of my cousins when he was five, and then Ginny. It worried me. If they were going to a better place then why was everyone crying?

Louise rolled down the window and the still-cool air rushed in, "I know the sun's coming up in the east but I don't know what's coming with it."

"Good times." Mother beamed.

"I don't know."

"Sis, good times." Mother smiled.

When Ginny took sick both Mother and Aunt Louise nursed her. Mother bore the full brunt of her sister's grief and she grieved, too, for Ginny was an exceptionally lovable person.

A long silence followed, then Louise drew in her breath, finally exhaling in one long stream. "I'm starting to feel old."

"Don't be silly. You're not a day over fifty-two."

"Forty-six," came the swift, icy reply.

"Ha."

"You'll always be my baby sister but don't make me older than I am." She shifted in her seat, rolling up the window because the air was brisk even though it was August. "Middle age is tricky. Some days I feel like I'm sixteen and other days, well. . . ." Her voice trailed off.

"I wouldn't know," came the saucy reply.

"Ha right back at you." Louise smiled broadly.

"You're only as old as you feel. Perk up."

"I try, Baby Sis, but sometimes things wash over me."

A silence followed. "Guess it does." Another moment passed and Mother added, "We have to fight back. In a way we have to live harder for Ginny. If you tart yourself up you'll feel better and younger. Really."

"Maybe, but I don't care if I bury my face in Pond's cold cream, the wrinkles are arriving."

"You look great."

Mother wasn't lying. Beautiful skin that aged slowly was a family trait. If anything, the men's skin glowed even fresher than the women's. Mother said shaving kept their skin smooth.

"You two look like twins." I added my two cents.

Mother, while grateful that I was mollifying her sister, shot me a fleeting glance. She liked being the baby and didn't want to look like Louise's twin.

"Aren't you sweet," Louise cooed.

The fog raised up enough so we could see the

landscape, flat as a pancake. The point of St. Mary's County lay right in front of us, what passed for a parking lot was crushed seashells. Beyond that the sands shifted with the winds, which fortunately were light.

Mother pulled onto the shells, tires crunching them, as the sun cleared the horizon. "Rise and shine."

I shook Leroy. "Wake up."

He opened his eyes, then sat up. "Look at all those birds. Aunt Wheezie, I have to go to the bathroom."

As Mother cut the motor, Louise opened the heavy car door, then opened the back door, and Leroy stepped out, his PF Flyers bright white because he'd scrubbed them with an S.O.S. pad. Leroy kept things organized and clean since his daddy insisted his son do chores in proper military fashion. I had to be organized, too.

"Honey, there's no one here so you go on over

14

there." She pointed to the edge of the shells. "Don't forget to shake."

Beet red, he mumbled, "Yes, Ma'am."

"I'm gonna look," I taunted.

Mother put her hand on my shoulder. "Nickel, don't be ugly."

"Mother, I've seen earthworms bigger than that."

"When did you see Leroy's part?" Aunt Louise's eyebrows shot up almost to her widow's peak.

"All the time. He always has to go to the bathroom." I shrugged because it didn't seem like a big deal to me.

Mother considered this, then patiently counseled, "Don't make fun of him. Boys, uh," she thought some more, "boys are very nervous about their part even if they brag about it."

Louise concurred. "They're very sensitive. I certainly hope he hasn't examined you." She enunciated "examined."

"Aunt Wheezie, he doesn't care about me at all. I don't want to see him but like I said, he's always going to the bathroom. I don't know why. I don't have to go to the bathroom that often."

They ignored my prattle as Mother opened the trunk of the car.

"I'll carry the hamper if you carry the big cooler." Louise reached for the cooler, the same one Dad used when he went pheasant hunting.

Mother without complaint lifted out the drinks cooler with a grunt. She knew Louise's back often hurt.

"Mother, Leroy says his part hurts sometimes. Why is that?"

"Fills with blood."

This sounded awful. "Should he go to the doctor?"

Both sisters laughed, then Louise said, "No."

"I don't see blood."

"Nickel, this is a discussion for another day," Mother suggested, which meant to shut up.

I couldn't argue, though I did say, "Well, I'm glad I don't have that problem."

"I am, too." Mother walked across the sand, her arms extended because the cooler was heavily loaded with drinks.

Louise followed with the hamper. "You wait for Leroy and then bring the blankets and my bag of tools. We're going to pick the perfect spot."

I leaned against the side of the car, the side away from Leroy, and when he whistled and returned, I lifted out a blanket and handed it to him. I took another blanket and picked up the plumber's bag, then closed the trunk. Inside the canvas plumber's bag were trowels, small buckets, a tin measuring cup, a T-square, popsicle sticks, pieces of colored paper, twine, scissors, a whittling knife, and a bottle of nail polish. He followed me toward where Mother and Aunt Louise stood, right hands shading their eyes.

Mother turned and motioned for us to hurry.

Once there, Louise pointed to the water, "Look at that."

A school of small fish were jumping out of the water, the sun turning their silver bodies red.

"Wow," Leroy held the blanket to his chest.

"Gotta be a shark or something pushing them." Mother studied nature and could identify birds and birdsongs, animals, trees, wildflowers. She taught me these things, including the different cries for mating, defending territory, and the "just plain happy" cry as she called it.

Leroy hugged the blanket tighter, "I'm not going in the water."

"Not now anyway. Sunrise is breakfast time for everyone and your little toes would look so tasty." Mother teased him.

"I'll keep my sneakers on," he replied solemnly.

Louise laughed, bending down to kiss his

cheek. "Don't do that. By the time the water warms up you'll be safe."

He nodded but clearly did not believe this.

"Who's hungry?" Mother took Leroy's blanket and spread it out.

Louise spread out my blanket and within minutes ham biscuits, cheese, little apple tarts, and deviled eggs graced the center of the blankets.

Mother poured hot tea for herself and me. Aunt Louise liked coffee, as did Leroy, so they drank from her green thermos, which had thin red concentric pin stripes. Co-colas and 7 UPs nestled in the cooler since no one in our family could survive long without one or the other. Occasionally, Mother would knock back a jigger of whiskey followed by a Co-cola but not often. When she did it was usually in winter after she'd trudged in from finishing her chores. No one in our family was a drinker except for PopPop, who came back from Verdun a changed man. He was good to me and let me sleep with his foxhounds as well as play with them—but sleeping with them was the big prize. Mother and Louise said he was never the same after the war. He drank off and on but when he was on, he'd drink a fifth of whiskey a day. Yet the minute he knew I was coming to stay with him he stopped. I didn't understand it.

Uncle Ken seemed the same after World War II, at least on the outside. Louise said that Ginny told her he'd wake up crying in the middle of the night. I never saw it myself. It was kind of funny, too, because he was proud to be a marine but said over and over he never wanted Leroy to go to war.

Once I told Uncle Ken I wanted to fight.

He put his hand on my shoulder and leaned down to whisper, "You would, too, but put it out of your mind."

Mother and Louise talked about the fall clothing coming into the department store on the downtown square. The colors proved a big topic, with Mother liking the plaids and Aunt Louise getting particular about what kind of plaid.

Since at that point I didn't know the difference between clan MacLeod and the tartan of the clan Lamont, I focused on Leroy. "You think a shark will eat you?"

"How about a manta ray?" His blue eyes widened.

"Too far north."

"How do you know?" he challenged me.

"Cause I read *National Geographic,* that's why."

He whispered, ham biscuit crumbs on his rosy lips, "Aunt Louise won't let me read it. Naked women. I saw one once and she had rings around her neck and her neck was long as a giraffe. No clothes hardly." He then covered his mouth with his hand and giggled.

I whispered back, "I saw that issue, too."

Mother had taught me to say, "issue" for periodicals. A stickler for proper identification of everything, she'd bang on me until I got it right.

"Cow udders." He giggled louder.

I whispered louder as I looked down at my flat chest, "If I grow lung warts like that I will die. Really and truly, Leroy, I will die."

We both turned our eyes to look at Mother and Aunt Louise's breasts which stood out nicely in their camp shirts, they each had a light sweater thrown over their shoulders, pressed shorts on their shapely legs. Men always looked at their legs so I guessed they were special. Then we giggled more.

"What are you two giggling about?" Mother reached over to playfully swat my head.

"Nothing," I lied, and we laughed even harder.

This made Mother and Aunt Louise laugh and then we all laughed although by now we didn't know why. It didn't matter.

"Juts, remember Aunt Doney's bathing suit?"

This brought on a war whoop from Mother, who laughed anew. "Oh, my God." She wiped her eyes with a napkin. "Kids, Aunt Doney wore this bathing suit that had to be from the 1880s if it was a day. Well, the darn thing was wool. I mean your Aunt Doney and Uncle Jim could afford a new bathing suit but, well, that's another story. She walked into the Bay. . . ."

"And the waves hit the shore." Aunt Louise dabbed her eyes because Aunt Doney was big as a house, the only family member who turned to fat.

Mother laughed more, then returned to the tale, "So she's out there paddling around and finally she comes on in. The day was right hot and to make a long story short, the suit shrunk. Whole sections of Aunt Doney hung over the edges of the suit. She about had a fit."

"Did it itch?" I wondered.

"Yeah and cut the circulation off her legs and arms so Uncle Jim told her she had to take it off, but there wasn't a place to change or wash up. But there was a nice big bucket by the outdoor pump, so we trundled over there. Louise and I had to hold up blankets so no one could see, and she stripped off the bathing suit, washed with the bucket. She'd pump and pump, pump and pour. There was a lot to wash. We're holding the blankets and remember, we're not much bigger than you all and our arms grew weary. Uncle Jim hurried to fetch her frock, as he called it. Before he got back to us this wind whipped in right off the Bay and we couldn't hold onto the blankets which were bigger than we were. Honey, there stood Aunt Doney just screaming and hollering vowing to kill us on the spot."

"I didn't know Uncle Jim could run that fast." Louise cried from laughter.

"If she'd kept her trap shut a few people would have noticed a large white lady naked by the water pump but no, she has to scream bloody murder and everyone on the beach witnessed all that jelly flab quivering."

They leaned on one another shoulder to

shoulder, laughing. One would subside, then the other would start up. They were worse than Leroy and me.

It was good to see Aunt Louise laugh.

"What she do to you?" Leroy, cautious of punishment, put down his ham biscuit.

"She made us go sit on the bench telling us we couldn't swim in the Bay. We were supposed to sit there until the mule jitney came by to carry us back to the train depot." Mother smiled at the memory.

"Did you?"

"Well. . . ," Mother fudged, since she didn't want Leroy and I to know what a devil she was, except we knew because not much had changed, she was just bigger, that's all.

"Your mother told everyone who passed by that an evil fat lady had forced us to sit on the green bench in the searing heat. We were going to dry up and fall down. Oh, it was a pitiful performance."

Breathlessly Leroy asked, "What happened?"

"A nice gentleman walked to the police station and the policeman came by on his horse to see what was doing. Juts really pulled out the stops so he took us to the station and we got cleaned up by the lady behind the desk. We were full of sand. And then they gave us ice cream." Aunt Louise relished the story.

"And they arrested Aunt Doney for cruelty to children." Mother laughed so hard she had to hold onto Louise or she'd tump over.

"It was a mess, I can tell you that, and Uncle Jim had to pay a fine and then he paid them more to keep it out of the papers. Great day." Louise drew out "day" in the Southern manner.

Aunt Doney didn't talk to us the whole way home, and that was a long train ride, I can tell you." Mother again wiped tears from her eyes.

"What did your Mama do when you got home?" Leroy's shoulders hunched up, already worried.

"She laughed and laughed. Aunt Doney got so

mad at her she didn't speak to her for a whole month and Mama said it was a blessed relief." Louise leaned on her sister again.

"It wasn't our fault a big wind came up." Mother's chin jutted out for a moment.

"Wasn't our fault she ate so much pie and cake, either. That woman could eat, eat like a farmhand. She didn't eat like that in public but when it was just us, she used her fork like a shovel. I vowed I would never look like that when I sat down at the table." For emphasis Louise again patted her lips with her cloth napkin.

"You don't eat much, Louise. Your prayer of thanks takes so long the food gets cold. You lose your appetite." Mother teased her.

"Juts, you're such a Philistine."

"What's a Philistine?" Leroy asked.

Aunt Louise removed her sweater as the sun climbed higher, dissipating the dawn clamminess. "What do they teach you at St. Patrick? You don't know what a Philistine is?"

"Apparently, it's me." Mother's red lipstick accentuated her grin.

"Juts." Louise used her schoolmarm tone.

"Jesus didn't like them," I volunteered.

"Your Aunt Louise doesn't like them," Mother said, a devilish lilt to her voice.

"All right, mock me if you must, but these children need to learn." She waited a moment, drama building in her mind at least. "The Philistines used to live in southwest Palestine and they made war on the ancient Israelites. But to call someone a Philistine means they're vulgar, common, that they only care about material things."

"Oh, like Mrs. Mundis." I inhaled the odor of the Bay, slightly saline at Point Lookout.

"Now, now." Louise sounded very charitable but really she liked my comment because Claudia Mundis had more money than God, and seemed intent on spending it.

"You know, Sis, she's almost finished with her new garden home."

"She's just nouveau riche and there's no two ways about it," Aunt Louise sighed.

"Better nouveau riche than no riche at all." Mother fished for a Chesterfield in her straw bag, found it, then dropped a line to find her lighter.

"Blood tells."

"For Christ's sake, Louise, not that again."

"Our family landed in Maryland in 1634 with Leonard Calvert. That landing became St. Mary's City and here we are in St. Mary's County." Aunt Louise threw out her chest, which was impressive.

"And it never put a penny in my pocket." Mother glanced overhead as a flock of terns zipped along. "Isn't it something how every bird is different and every kind of bird is perfect for what it has to do? I love watching."

Mother hated the Southern snottiness over genealogy. Dad's family arrived in Virginia in 1620. He never once mentioned it although his mother trumpeted this deathless information loud and clear. Maybe their disdain for blood arrogance was one of the ties that bound them.

By seven-thirty the lovely beach started to fill. Colorful umbrellas were stuck in the sand, and blankets were spread out, big striped towels folded to the side. Everyone toted a hamper. Leroy and I noted no kids our age. We weren't going to play with babies, the worst. The teenagers thought the same thing about us.

"I'm going for a swim." Mother stood up, stepped out of her shorts and took off her white camp shirt. Her one-piece bathing suit was a pretty melon color, and showed off her figure. Mother could turn heads. She gloried in it.

"I'll be down in a minute." Louise affixed a floppy straw hat to her curls. She loved hats.

I jumped up to race after Mother, then stopped, "Come on, Leroy."

"No. Sharks. I saw those fish jumping."

"Ah, that was a long time ago. Come on."

"Nope."

"Crabs will get you," I threatened him, and as if to prove my point along sidled a little blue crab. "See."

"Better a crab than a shark."

"Chicken."

"Philistine." He grinned using that big word.

This set Aunt Louise off which pleased Leroy even more.

Just as Mother stepped into the water, which was still cold, I splashed by her, getting water all over. She squinted, then bent over and threw water on me.

"You're all wet, kid."

"You, too." I loved Mother.

It wasn't until later in my school years that I realized some children don't love their mothers or fathers. Course when you met their parents you understood why.

She reached out for me and took my hand. "Come on."

We waded out until my feet couldn't touch bottom, but she'd lift me up every time a swell rolled in. When the water reached her bosoms, she held me with both hands.

"How deep is it, Mother?"

"How tall am I?"

"Uh, six feet."

She laughed, "Nickel, I'd be taller than Dad. He's five ten. Try again."

"Five feet."

"Close, kid, but no cigar." She still had her Chesterfield dangling from her mouth but it was burning down fast.

I considered Mother's cigarette a fashion accoutrement.

"Five two?"

"Bingo. So how deep is it? Think about how tall I am and how high the water is. Use your head."

"Maybe four feet."

"Maybe you're right." She smiled, then carried me back until my feet could touch. "You can almost always figure things out if you look around. That's the trouble with most people, honey, they listen to what other people tell them or they stick their nose in the sand. Use your head."

"Daddy always says, 'Put your money in your head, no one can steal it from you there.'"

She smiled, "He's full of sayings. Usually right." She turned around to glance back at the beach. "For Christ's sake, Louise is sitting there putting on lotion. One freckle will send her to the emergency room."

"She doesn't have freckles."

"That's the point." Mother released my hand. "I wish I had the money my sister spends on potions."

"Perfumes, Aunt Wheezie has more perfumes than anyone."

"She does, doesn't she?"

"How come she called you a Philistine?"

"Oh, she was joking. She didn't mean it ugly. I could have gotten even and called her a Pharisee."

"Jesus didn't like them either." Bible school had some effect on me and I'd heard the word but I didn't know exactly what a Pharisee was. Just like I'd heard the word "eucharist" but didn't exactly know what it meant.

"Hypocrites. A Pharisee is a hypocrite, praying loudly in public and then doing whatever he wants when no one is looking."

"Is Aunt Wheezie really a Pharisee?"

"Well . . . no, but she's sure trying to rub the Bible off on everyone and she's not perfect. Ever since Ginny died she's turned into a religious nut." Mother stared at me, then touched my shoulder. "It's horrible to lose a daughter. I try to remember that when I get mad at her or when she starts being more Catholic than the Pope." She cupped her hands, lifting water that was clear, then opened them and watched it fall back into the Bay. "Time. She'll leave off bleeding Jesus in time."

"Mother, you know when you kneel next to me when I say my prayers?"

"Yes."

"I don't want to say that prayer anymore."

"The Lord's Prayer?" This surprised her.

"No. I don't want to say, 'Now I lay me down to sleep, I pray the Lord my soul to keep; if I should die before I wake, I pray the Lord my soul to take.'"

She pursed her lips, ready to say something, then stopped herself. "I see."

"When Aunt Ginny died Leroy and I didn't want to say that prayer anymore but we were scared to say anything."

"You're not scared now."

"Time." I smiled up at her.

"Aren't you the smart little thing?" She considered this. "Well, we have to find another prayer. You could recite one of the Psalms, they're pretty. You like most of them. And you read them very well for your age."

"I'll do a Psalm."

"What about Leroy?"

"He's afraid to talk to Aunt Wheezie since she's gotten so . . . you know."

"I'll see what I can do." She reached for my hand again. "You've kept this to yourself all this time? Every night you say that prayer. That's a long time, half a year, to do something you don't like." She dropped my hand, looking out over the Bay. "Funny, Nickel, sometimes I wish I had your discipline. You came into the world with it. I struggle with it."

"You work hard." I equated work with discipline.

"Root hog or die." She laughed. "I mean you can control your feelings. Pretty much what's inside comes outside for me. Louise, too, although she can hang on longer than I can." She looked over at her sister again. "Now she's building a sand castle with Leroy. Those two are a lot alike in some ways. Artistic." She turned back, casting her eyes over the seemingly infinite expanse of water. "The Bay has magical powers. The Indians who lived here thought so. There's no other place like this in the world. It's fed by God knows how many streams and small rivers, which then flow into the five main ones. Know what they are?"

"The Potomac, uh, the James." I was stuck.

She filled in, "The York, the Rappahannock, and the Susquehanna. Someday when you're grown, think about today. I bet you have a car then and you can drive here and feel the magic all over again. Spirits guard the waters. I swear it's true but don't say anything to Louise. She'll think it's blasphemous. Maybe it is but I believe in spirits and in angels and in devils." She pushed water at me. "I'm looking at a little devil right now."

"Not me."

"Right." She reached for my hand. "Come on, kid, let's go up and help build the sand castle or she'll get her nose out of joint."

"Aunt Wheezie doesn't like the water?"

"She likes the water fine, she just doesn't want to get her hair wet."

"Oh." Mine was slicked back wet. "Can I get a flattop like Leroy's? Then I won't have to comb my hair."

"No."

"I'd have more time to do the dishes and chores. Think how much time I waste combing my hair."

She laughed. "You're going to grow up to be a politician."

"Is that a good thing?"

"No, but it runs in the family. It helps if you can talk out of both sides of your mouth at the same time."

Taking this literally, I tried, and this made her laugh harder.

"Can't do it."

"Don't worry about it now." She squeezed my hand and we dripped our way up to the others. We toweled off, careful not to sprinkle one drop onto Louise's blanket.

The thick outer walls of the sand castle loomed up, squared off. Louise fretted over the towers at the corners. Her skill and the speed at which she worked amazed me. Leroy mixed sand and water in a bucket to the correct consistency.

Building things also ran in the family. Both sisters loved designing garden sheds, little forcing sheds, a new garage with living quarters over top. They threw themselves into the actual work. Mother had a miter box, a good saw, and an array of tools neatly hung up on her workroom wall, itself another one of her practical designs.

Soon the two sisters labored over the elaborate sand castle while Leroy and I filled two small buckets with sand and water. We wore a path down to the Bay and back. After a while the buckets grew heavy.

We began to carry one bucket together, slowing the builders down.

"How many more of these do they need?" Leroy's green swimming trunks flapped in the breeze.

"A million."

"You lie."

"I don't know." I answered. "Twenty?"

"Aunt Wheezie said we'd build a sand castle but all I'm doing is hauling this bucket."

"Ah, Leroy, you know how she gets."

"Yeah."

We delivered the bucket to them, setting it down in unison.

"Mother, we're going to take a walk." That seemed the wiser course than saying we were tired and bored with carrying sand and water.

"Okay." She cheerfully agreed while Louise created turrets at the top of the castle walls.

"Don't be too long. I'll need more buckets," Louise finally spoke, eyes still on her turrets.

"Yes, Ma'am."

As we started off I heard Mother say, "I'll get the sand. Those kids have hauled plenty."

"Good for 'em." Louise meticulously cut into the sand wall to make the turret square.

"Let them be kids."

"We worked."

"Not hauling sand for sand castles. They do their part." Mother noticed I was looking back and she winked.

I reached for Leroy's hand but he pulled it away. "I'm no baby."

"You're a cootie."

PopPop, who fought in World War I, told us about cooties. We also had a game called cootie, where'd you'd roll dice and, according to the number, get a plastic piece of a bug. The winner was the one who put together the cootie first. It always provoked a fight.

"Then you're a nit. That's ten times worse than a cootie."

"Dung dot."

"Cow pie."

"Steaming dog turd." My imagination was waking up.

His blue eyes widened and he slugged my shoulder. "Asshole."

"Hey." I slugged him back.

Being even we continued our walk, oblivious to the people who were equally oblivious to us.

"When I'm grown up you won't dare hit me."

"You say."

"I'll be bigger and stronger."

"Could be, but I'll always be faster and smarter."

He echoed my words, "You say."

"I do say."

"You broke your Lent, how smart is that?"

Lent seemed light years back and I did break it. "So?"

"You'll go to hell."

"Because I ate chocolate?"

"You broke your Lent." He stubbornly clung to reciting my downfall.

"What does Jesus need with my chocolate?"

"Doesn't matter. A promise is a promise."

"You made me do it." I flared up for a second.

"I did not."

"Did, too. You ate a Snickers right in front of me."

"You're supposed to be strong."

"You know, Leroy, you're turning into a religious nut just like Aunt Wheezie."

Since his mother died, Leroy was living with Louise. When Ken got off work they'd all eat together and then Ken would go to bed. He was worn out.

"You don't believe anything," he responded. His blond hair, crew cut, seemed almost white in the sunshine.

"I go to church," I said, but he was hitting the nail on the head because even at seven I evidenced little passion for organized religion.

"Not the one true church."

"You gonna be a priest or something?"

"I dunno." The sass leached out of him. "Aunt Louise would like that. I'd like to be a marine like Dad. Dad says they give you a place to live, you get clothes and food. I'd like that. I like to march."

"You have to do what other people tell you to do."

"Do that now." A note of resignation filled his little voice.

"Me, too, but it won't always be like this. We can do what we want once we're grown up."

"I like to fish. It's quiet." We walked along and then he asked, "What do you want to do?"

"Ride horses. Play with PopPop's hounds."

"You have to make money when you're big."

It surprised me that Leroy was thinking about that.

"I can make money riding horses and I can clean kennels. I like to muck out things. They look so pretty when I'm done."

"Not me." He wrinkled his nose. "That's why I want to be a marine. I get all that stuff like I said but they pay you, too. Dad said he saved a lot of money when he was in the service."

"Yeah, but you have to go to war."

"Only if there's a war." He thought about this. "Dad says it's bad. I shouldn't do it. War. But it can't be so bad because he's real proud to be a marine." He stopped. "You could be a marine."

"No horses." I couldn't live without horses.

"Oh."

I opened my hand, a quarter rested in my palm. "See. This is why I was going to hold your hand. I was going to give you the quarter and we could buy ice cream."

Dismay crossed his regular features, he paused, then scooped the quarter out of my hand and ran like a scalded dog for the ice cream stand.

I ran after him, almost overtaking him a few strides before we ducked under the wide red-and-white striped awning.

He giggled. "Couldn't catch me."

"Let you win. I want a rocky road."

He ordered two scoops of chocolate and my rocky road. We sat on a bench and happily ate our ice cream cones. Then we washed up at the pump, probably the same pump where Aunt Doney exposed all.

"We'd better go back." I pumped more water for him to wash his face.

"I don't want to carry more buckets."

"I'll carry the buckets. It's easier if you carry one in each hand, anyway. I don't care."

He sighed. "Okay."

The water tickled our toes as we walked slowly back toward Mother and Aunt Louise. Hermit crabs scuttled about and a bald eagle flew overhead, so big it made me blink. Little birds ran on the sand, their legs a blur of motion.

I stopped to pluck up a hermit crab. It sucked back into its small shell with a faint clatter.

"I don't like crabs."

"Me neither but I like hermits. Must be hard work carrying your house on your back."

"How can you tell a girl crab from a boy crab?"

"Girl crabs have prettier shells."

"Not true." He poked me.

I put the crab down where it prudently remained in its shell. "Big crabs? Not hermits?"

"Yeah, how do you tell?"

"She-crabs have round bellies. Male crabs, jimmies, have triangular bellies."

He wiggled his toes each time the water ran up over his feet. "Means you have to get close and tip them over to look."

"Not if you have good eyes."

"I have good eyes but I'm not gonna get close enough to a crab to look."

"Then why'd you ask?"

He shrugged with no reply so I said, "It's better than other animals maybe."

"What?"

"Their parts."

"Why is it better if you have to get close to see?"

"Better because stuff doesn't hang out. If you

47

didn't have your bathing trunks on you'd be, uh . . ." I thought hard for the word, "dangling. I mean a birdie could swoop right out of the sky and bite you. Think you're a big worm."

His face flushed. "Would not."

"I can see it now." I waved to the birds overhead. "Worm! Worm!"

He hunched his shoulders, "Better not." His hand covered his crotch.

"See. It would be awful." I laughed.

"Better than sitting down to pee." He brightened at his superiority in this department.

"Yeah."

"Better than having a baby and looking like a cow."

"Maybe." The appeal of becoming a mother eluded me at seven although some of my girlfriends played with dolls endlessly, in dress rehearsal.

"So. I'm not a worm."

"I didn't say you were a worm. I said your part

looks like a worm to a bird. A great big fat night crawler." How I enjoyed tormenting him.

"Take your nose first."

I felt my nose. "Still there. Doesn't wiggle when I walk. See, that's why the bird will grab you."

"Got my trunks on. Can't see."

"If I pulled your trunks down, it'd be gone. Pfft. God, Leroy, then you'd have to sit down to pee."

He considered this, being a serious sort, then it dawned on him that I didn't mean it. "I'd pee on you."

"Cootie."

"Pissant."

"You're the pissant. You just said you'd pee on me." I kicked up water from the edge. "I'd knock you sideways."

"You and what army?" He boasted idly, knowing full well I could whoop him good.

I stooped, jaw slightly ajar. "Look."

His eyes traveled in the direction of my own. "Golly Ned."

Mother and Aunt Louise had used colored paper cut in small triangles and toothpicks. The bits of paper, shaped like pennants, were taped to the ends of the toothpicks and stuck into the corner towers. Materials for the drawbridge rested next to the empty bucket.

"It's beautiful."

He nodded. "We don't have to carry any more buckets."

Louise, on hands and knees, big hat tipped down, lifted her head as we approached. "Need another bucket of sand and water."

Leroy picked up the bucket and handed it to me.

"Cootie," I said under my breath.

"Fly poop," he said under his.

I took my time filling the bucket, achieving the correct texture of sand and water. Fortified by my rocky road ice cream it didn't seem as heavy.

"Put it there." Louise pointed to the front of

the castle where she'd drawn two lines in the sand with her T-square.

"Aunt Wheezie, this castle is your best one yet." I meant that.

"Hey, what about me?" Mother put her thumb on the bottom of a popsicle stick, her forefinger on the top, and flicked it at me.

"You, too, Mother."

Leroy reposed on the blanket.

"Why don't you go for a swim, honey? Cool off?" Mother encouraged him.

"No."

"Fraidy cat," I taunted him.

"I'd rather be a fraidy cat than have fishies eat me."

"Balls."

"Nickel, where'd you hear such a word?" said Mother, who used it not infrequently at home.

I opened, then closed, my mouth.

"That's enough talk like that, young lady." Louise frowned.

"Yes, Ma'am. I'm sorry." Young though I was I had already developed a keen sense of the battles I might lose as well as the ones I might win.

"Leroy," Louise pointed her trowel at him. "The fish aren't going to eat you. Don't go out too far."

"No." He glowered.

"Just go in up to your waist." She kept at him.

"What waist?" I countered.

"Will you stay out of this?" Louise shot me a hot look.

"Nickel, you dig the moat and I'll put together the drawbridge." Mother reached for more popsicle sticks.

"Do I have to dig it all the way around?"

"Lazy," came the terse reply, which meant I'd have to do it or suffer endless descriptions to all and sundry about how slothful I was.

Down on my knees digging I called to Leroy. "Come on."

"She didn't ask me."

"I'm asking you."

"No."

"Who's lazy?" I pleaded to Mother.

"Root hog or die." She used the expression again.

"That means Leroy should work."

Neither Mother nor Louise, heads bent over their tasks, replied.

"I picked potato bugs." Leroy, feeling his popularity dipping with everyone, defended himself.

"You did a good job." Louise kept a large garden at her large house.

"I picked more than Nickel."

"You did not, you liar."

"That's enough." Mother, voice low, warned.

Frustrated I dug faster.

"Careful where you throw that sand. Pile it up so I can use it," Louise ordered.

"Leroy, you can at least haul this sand down to the water and mix it up." I loathed him at this point.

"No."

I stood, picked up the bucket, walked to the blanket and threw the sand at him. "Move your lazy ass!"

He jumped up and socked me. I pasted him right back.

Louise grabbed Leroy while Mother pulled me off him. Although a few months younger I was quicker and stronger than my cousin.

"Girls shouldn't fight." He spit at me, face red.

"That's right, Leroy. Just sit on the blanket."

This enraged him further. He lunged for me, throwing Louise off balance. She almost fell into her creation.

"Wheezie, take him for a swim. Nick and I will keep working on this."

Usually not one to take counsel from her kid sister, Louise surprised all of us by doing just that.

"Leroy, come with me."

"I don't want to."

"You're going with me or you're going to sit in that car and fry. Do you hear me?"

"Yes, Ma'am."

Reluctantly he followed her into the water.

"Why is he such a pill? He didn't used to be like that. I hate him. I really do." I returned to my chore making fast work of it.

Mother lashed the popsicle stick together with twine to make a drawbridge, her fingers nimble and working in a rhythm. "I don't know, kid. When you're little—seven or eight is still little compared to Wheezie and I," she said, remembering how we hated to be thought little, "you've got lots of time to figure things out. You might hurt now but it will ease up in time. You and Leroy don't know that yet. When you hurt it fills you up. Might take him years to come back to his old jolly self."

"He wasn't jolly."

"All right then, fun."

I kept digging and thinking. "Why does he take it out on me?"

She blew air out of her nostrils, "Because he loves you."

"That doesn't make any sense." My ruthless logic did not always serve me well, then or now.

"Honey," she put down her mostly finished drawbridge, "he knows you'll bear it. He's mad at the world and you're the only one he can beat on. He can't beat on his daddy. God knows, Ken is worse off than Leroy. Right now there's a big black hole in both their hearts and it's just full of pain. I know it upsets you and I know you have that hot temper. Count to ten, then count to ten again."

"I'll try."

"I know you will. For a brat, you're a good kid," she smiled mischievously.

"Were you a brat?"

"Still am according to Her Holiness." Mother nodded toward Louise, who looked fetching in her baby blue bathing suit.

"You ever hit her?"

"Well, sure. Used to drive Mama crazy." She picked up the drawbridge, knotting the ends of the twine then to hang it from the castle's front door. "Mama died in 1947. You remember her a little bit, don't you?"

"I remember Big Wheezie," I said, and I did. "I don't remember her dying."

"You weren't there when she passed. None of us were. She was shelling peas on the front porch and she had a heart attack." She put down the drawbridge and snapped her fingers. "Just like that. Tell you what, that's the way to go. Fast."

"I don't want to die."

"I don't expect anyone does unless the pain gets so bad you don't want to live, either. There comes a time for some people when there's not a scrap of joy left in life and they're ready to go. But what I'm getting at is that that was five years ago and I think of my mother every day, and more than once. If I live to one hundred, I'll think of my mother. You do roll on over the hurt, finally, but you never forget, and you know, you never stop loving that person."

"Mom," I rarely called her that, "you aren't fixing to die, are you?"

She smiled, her even teeth white despite the endless succession of Chesterfields, proof of the benefits of brushing your teeth hard with baking soda. "Not any time soon. I think I'll make Death chase me down."

"Like the old man with the scythe?"

"Right. He's going to have to swing and run at the same time." With her fingers she put a screw on one side of the top of the opening where the drawbridge would go. "Wish I had a winch."

"Ma'am?" I'd been strictly raised so "Huh?" wouldn't cut it.

"A winch, you know, a round small drum with teeth. The size depends on what you have to haul. Drawbridges were raised and lowered from inside with a huge winch that one man, or sometimes two, turned. I could have made one from an empty spool of thread. Mmm, maybe something bigger."

"I don't think anyone will notice. They'll just see this big castle."

"I'll notice." She hung the drawbridge, closing the opening, then she carefully dropped it down, palm under the popsicle sticks, until it rested on the sand over my moat. "There."

"You can build anything."

"I can. If I had money to burn I'd always have something in the works. I'd love to build a stone addition to our house. That will be a cold day in hell." She sighed, then smiled. "Sometimes I think it's our wants that keep us alive."

"Aunt Wheezie says you are very materialistic but she's spiritual."

Mother's lustrous gray eyes narrowed, "Balls."

I neglected to point out that she'd uttered the very word for which I'd just been chastised. "That's what she says."

"Goddamned religious nut is what she is. More Catholic than the pope. Of course he has a better wardrobe but she spends a bundle on clothes. Have you ever seen your Aunt Wheezie looking like anything but a million bucks?"

"No, but you always look prettier." This wasn't idle flattery, because Mother was a wee bit flashier than her older sister.

"Thank you, honey." She just ate it up. "Let me tell you about my dear big sis. First, I love her to death. Second, she can be a Pharisee. If I'm the Philistine, well, she's the Pharisee. She can be the biggest goddamned hypocrite. She's plenty wrapped up in jewelry, cars, clothes. Her house. Do you know what her dining room table is worth? It's a Hepplewhite. People know about Sheraton and Chippendale but this is as good, if not better, and the damned thing is two hundred years old and then some. Chairs, too. Sanctimonious twit. If I had those damned chairs, I could pay off the farm."

"How come she's rich?"

Mother sat down, took the little gardening hand shovel from my hand because I'd completed my task. "She married money. Pearlie," Uncle Paul's nickname was "Pearlie," "wasn't born with a silver spoon in his mouth but his family had some money, and I have to give her credit, she helped him build the business."

"Is that why she's in her office all the time?"

Mother nodded. "She keeps the books, she makes the purchases, she calls clients, she puts the ads in the newspapers—we design those together. She works hard. She's got a business head, always did."

Uncle Pearl owned the largest painting company along the Mason-Dixon Line from Hagerstown in Maryland to York in Pennsylvania, and it had a reputation for excellent work and fair pricing. Sometimes museums used him because he knew so much about old paints as so many of the houses he worked on had been built in the mid-seventeenth century and then enlarged, usually in the eighteenth century. Going through an old house with Uncle Pearlie on a job bid thrilled me. I'd already inherited the building and rebuilding bug from Mother, and Uncle Pearlie had taught me how to really look at a structure.

Dad, not a driven kind of guy, still worked for his father, a man not known for generosity. But Dad would inherit the dry goods store someday so he dutifully kept at it, which drove Mother nuts. We also farmed and Mother did most of that work. She could drive a tractor better than the men.

"You keep Dad's books."

"Only the house. His mother will give up her bookkeeping when she dies. We'll have to pry those double-entry account books from her frozen fingers, the old bitch." She reached for her pack of Chesterfields, resting on top of the wide castle wall, the matches next to it. "Thank God for the Indian and tobacco." She lit up.

"May I have a puff?"

The cigarette, lipstick already on the end, glowed as she breathed in. "Don't inhale a lot, hear me? Just a tiny little intake and don't let Her Holiness see you. Turn your back."

I bent over and she cupped her hands around the fag as I inhaled what to me was a little. Burning tendrils snaked down into my lungs. My eyes watered.

Mother laughed, "Blow it out, kid, or you'll bust a gut."

I exhaled more from relief than anything. "Jeez!"

"Gotta learn to do it, and it's not the smartest thing to do, I'll grant you that." She inhaled deeply, her eyes closed, bliss emanating from her body. "Ahhh." She blew silver-blue smoke from her nose, which I loved to see. "Here's the deal, kid: it's a nasty habit. Colors your teeth so you have to go to the dentist more often, though brushing with baking soda helps. Turns your fingers yellow.

Gotta chew mints because your breath will smell like an ashtray, plus it gets into all your clothes and the house smells like old smoke, all stale."

"Why do you do it?"

She pulled her knees up to her chin, circling them with her arms, cigarette between forefinger and middle finger. "Relaxes me. Kind of gives me a little jolt at the same time. But mostly I can think better. You know, everyone will try to live your life for you. Here I am just about forty-seven and my big sister still tells me what to do."

I interrupted, not very proper but I did it. "Dad doesn't tell you what to do."

"He knows better."

"How can you can get Dad to listen but not Aunt Wheezie?"

She sucked in another long drag. "Any woman worth her salt can get just about any man to do what she wants. Of course, the longer you're married the more ingenuity it takes."

"How?"

"Kid, that's a subject for a later date. Back to fags." She held up her cigarette between us. "Like I said, people will try to live your life for you. You gotta fight back. If this damned cigarette brings me a little pleasure, so what about the rest of it? Is it unhealthy? Well, I expect it is but I have to die sometime."

"You said you weren't going to die." A wave of panic hit me.

"Not now," she laughed. "Actually, I'd better not say that. Here today; gone tomorrow. But the odds are, I'll be around for a long time. I fully intend to live long enough to be a burden to you."

"Maybe you're a burden now." I'd picked up some of Mother's quickness.

She choked from laughing. "You little shit."

"See. God's punishment."

"Oh." She rolled her eyes. "My own daughter. A religious nut. Christ, now we've got two in the family."

"Mother, I promise never to be a religious nut."

"I'll hold you to that." She dug in the sand with her toes, the red toenail polish calling attention to her dainty feet. "Just another bunch of people telling you what to do and how to do it. Nickel, that's not the same as believing. They're all a bunch of bullshitters and thieves."

"Not Aunt Wheezie."

"No, she's just . . . ah, well, she's gotten feverish about it. When Ginny first came down with the cancer Wheezie beat a path to her pew. She got calluses on her knees, though I can't blame her. She prayed herself hoarse." Mother's eyes glistened. "Didn't do a damn bit of good. God, how Ginny suffered. The first six months, well, it wasn't so bad but those last two. Honey," she lifted my chin with her left hand, "I hope you never suffer like that and I don't want to suffer either. If God loves us we'll die like Mama."

"God didn't love Ginny?"

"I don't know. She was the sweetest kid I've ever known. I used to tease Wheezie that she couldn't be her baby. Someone must have switched babies in the hospital. Course, Ginny was the spitting image of my sister." She twisted her cigarette in the sand, extinguishing it. "Takes a long, long time. Everyone looks okay on the outside but on the inside, it's there. That emptiness."

I jumped up and turned a cartwheel. "Does that help?"

Her eyes filled with tears. "It does." She wiped them away then looked down at the Bay. "That is the longest Wheezie has ever been in the water. She'll turn into a prune."

"Would fish really eat us?"

"Sure. Not now, though. Conditions would have to be right or wrong. A shark or some kind of big fish would have to come in close and I don't know why they come in sometimes and not others. I wonder if there are storms out in the Atlantic that we don't know about or currents are running harder underneath the water. All I know is sometimes big fish come calling. I figure they're always closer in around dawn and dusk. If you notice, most all creatures feed then except for the cattle and horses, they just keep walking and eating, walking and eating, all day. Anyway, you learn when to go in and when to stay out. But Leroy is in no danger from fish. Course, he's in danger from Louise trying to send him into the priesthood."

"Won't work."

"I think not."

"I wouldn't want to wear that white collar around my neck."

"You're safe." She picked up the tools, knocking off the sand, and replaced them in the canvas bag. "You know, it looks pretty good."

"Are you hungry?" I'd learned not to ask for food but to politely ask if the other person needed some.

"Getting there, which means you are." She checked her ladylike wristwatch. "Go on down there and move those two along. It'll take Wheezie twenty minutes to shower, remove every grain of sand from between her toes, put on espadrilles, and replenish her lipstick." She exhaled loudly. "It's a wonder she has a minute to call her own with all that primping."

"Aunt Wheezie says a woman must suffer for beauty."

"Actually, everyone around her suffers, too. Go on."

I ran down to the water's edge. "Aunt Wheezie, Mother says it's time for lunch."

She checked her own ladylike wristwatch, a much more expensive version than Mother's, the face so tiny and square she had to bring it right up to her eyes to tell time. "Hmm."

I scampered back up to Mother.

"What'd she say?"

"Hmm."

Within a few minutes the two of them rejoined us, Louise handing Leroy a towel.

"Wheeze, let's go to the crab place."

"Which one?"

"The one right on this side of St. Mary's. That's a good one," Mother replied, saying St. Mary's instead of St. Mary's City.

It wasn't really a city in 1952 but the word added importance.

"We have to leave our sand castle." Louise looked protectively at their creation.

"Sooner or later it will go."

"We built it far enough away from the water. High tide won't take it."

"Louise, it's made of sand. It gave us something to do." Then, seeing that this tack wasn't working, Mother said, "Remember that parable about the man who built his house on sand?"

A dark eyebrow arced suspiciously, "You quoting Scripture?"

"I'm not quoting, I'm remembering. You're the one always rubbing the Bible off on people."

"Juts, I am not rubbing the Bible off on people as you so crudely put it. I am trying to live a life as He would wish."

"Well, He got hungry, too. There was a Last Supper. All I want is a good lunch."

This seeming blasphemy exhausted Louise's reserves of Christian patience. "Don't you dare talk like that in front of these innocents."

She put her hands over Leroy's ears, a dramatic touch unappreciated by him.

"Sis, give up the cross. Other people need the wood."

"You are *impossible*. Impossible. You'll be languishing in purgatory for centuries."

"Balls."

"That's it. I've had it." Louise threw her stuff together, grabbed Leroy by the wrist and pulled him toward the car.

Mother, hands on hips, whistled a few notes from the hymn, "Holy, Holy, Holy."

Without turning her back, Louise, straight as a stick, threw everything in the trunk, got in the driver's seat and roared off.

"Mother, what are we going to do?"

"Wait until she comes back. She won't leave us here."

"But I'm hungry."

"Me, too." She sat down on her blanket, filled her hand with sand, then let it run between her fingers.

She laughed with a start. "She drove off before she dried off and changed out of her bathing suit. Ha. The driver's seat will be soaking wet and she has to drive home."

"How come?"

"Because I drove here. We take turns. She has to drive back. Don't you just love it?"

"Do you love Aunt Wheezie?"

"Not right this minute, I don't."

"How come you love someone sometimes and not others? I hate Leroy especially when he's a great big fat chicken. But I kinda love him."

"Oh, that's just how it is when people are close. If you have a friend you see, say, once a week, or even your friend at school, it's easier to get along with them than someone you have to live with day in and day out."

"Like Daddy?"

She smiled. "Daddy's pretty easygoing, thank God. Louise is not."

"Even when she was little?"

"Well," Mother thought for awhile, "she wanted to please a lot more than I did, and do. Even then she believed things, you know, believed people in charge. I might believe them and I might not. I had to think about it."

"You tell me to believe you." I enjoyed giving her a little dig.

"I'm your sainted mother." She grinned. "You know that commandment that says, 'Honor thy father and mother.'"

"What about Dinny Morton? Her mama is a drunk and you can smell her, too." My eyes widened with this bit of detail.

"That's hard. Hard." She lit another Chesterfield. "But when Dinny gets older she'll understand that Rachel"—she used Mrs. Morton's first name—"has an affliction. Drinking is a terrible curse. Rachel's father was a drunk, and his father too, and I guess they've always been drunks. Course, no one puts a gun to your head and says, 'You will knock back this bourbon and branch.' I don't see how they can stand the taste." Her lips turned down. "Just awful."

"I saw you drink champagne at Christmas."

"A sip. Champagne's not so bad but I plain don't like the taste and your father doesn't drink much either. A cold beer in hot weather is about it for him. Tell you what, I thank Jesus for that. Being married to a drunk is pure hell."

"What about communion. That's wine."

"A sip. Pretty awful, too."

"Do you really think it's the blood of Christ?" I had heard from Aunt Louise about transubstantiation, her own breathless version of the sacrament, which sounded like cannibalism to me.

"No."

"Then why do you do it?"

"To keep the peace. Sometimes, honey pie, you have to go along to get along. The trick is knowing when and where you can get away with just being yourself." She thrilled a long, deep drag. "Tell you something, my little chip off the old block, being yourself is the greatest luxury of all."

"Here she comes." I jumped up as the Nash stopped by the beach's edge.

"Told you. She can't live without me."

"Better not tell her that."

Mother rose, gathering her things, handing some to me to carry, "You have a wise old head on those young shoulders. Sometimes you surprise me." She tossed the short towel around her neck. "Just act as if nothing happened. Get in the back seat and shut your trap. She'll want to simmer a bit and she wants us to fully appreciate the depths of her forgiveness."

I did as I was told. Leroy kept quiet, too. The biggest surprise was neither sister spoke to the other until we reached the restaurant, a weathered clapboard shack with the ubiquitous white sign, a big red crab on front of it, swinging from a yardarm. Wooden picnic tables were neatly lined up outside under awnings and most were filled, as was the crushed shell parking lot.

Once she parked, Louise got out of the car, opened the trunk, pulled out her smaller towel, neatly folded it, and put it on the driver's seat. She then retrieved a little carry bag.

"I'm going to change. You can order for me." Louise started for the bathrooms.

"Okay. I'll change when you get back."

"What about me?" I asked because I hated sitting around in my bathing suit even when it was mostly dry.

"Let us go first then you can fix up."

When the rest of us were sitting down at a table in the back, under some nice trees, Mother picked up the rock on the table and handed us menus that had been underneath. Both Leroy and I could read a menu if it was simple. If it contained French words we were lost. This one, however, a mimeographed sheet run off daily, stuck to the basics: crab, sand dabs, clams, oysters, fried chicken or hotdogs for those who didn't like seafood, and cole slaw, fries, and hushpuppies.

"Little crabs eat one another. When they grow up they eat dead people," I helpfully informed Leroy.

"Do not."

"Pluck the eyes right out of their head, then they eat the nose and take big bites out of their cheeks. They just love dead people. So tasty."

"Nickel." Mother said simply.

"It's true."

"Is it true, Aunt Julia, is it?"

"Well, I wouldn't emphasize *people* but yes, crabs and lobsters are the Bay's cleanup crew."

"So they do eat dead people?" His voice was hushed.

"Now, Leroy, how many dead people do you think are in the Chesapeake Bay?" She hoped to lighten his mood.

Again, I proved helpful. "Thousands. Millions. We don't know how many Indians drowned in there before we came."

"Nickel, will you shut up?" Mother rarely used "shut up." She turned to Leroy. "Don't listen to her. Your cousin never heard a war story or a ship-wreck tale she didn't like. She has a penchant for violence." She cut her eyes and I understood that if I continued on my wayward conversational path the violence would be directed against myself.

Louise appeared, all smart in her halter top and pressed white shorts. Her soft yellow espadrilles matched her halter and she'd tied a navy blue bandanna around her hair.

"My turn." Mother left us.

"Has the waitress come yet?"

"No, Ma'am," I answered. "It's pretty busy."

"The best places always are." Louise studied the mimeographed sheet, the ink a soft purple. "I'm having softshell crabs, fries, and the world's biggest Co-cola. What about you all?"

"Hotdog." Leroy said quietly.

"That's it?"

"He's afraid to eat a crab," I volunteered.

"Why, Leroy?"

"I am not. I don't like crabs."

"He knows they eat dead people."

"Not the ones you'll be eating," she replied glibly.

"How can you tell?" Leroy truly was fretting over the image of a crab plucking out eyes.

"I just can," came the not very specific reply.

"I want a hotdog with mustard and a Co-cola."

"Leroy, the Chesapeake Bay is famous for soft-shell crabs. Won't get another chance to eat them until next summer. The season starts the first full moon in May and ends in September. It's almost September."

"Aunt Wheezie, I want a hotdog. Really." He closed his mouth, which became a straight line.

"Chicken," I whispered, to further torment him.

He turned to me but stopped as Louise said, "Chicken? Don't tell me you don't want to eat softshell crabs either? What about oysters? Last year two and a half million oysters were hauled up out of the Bay. But this is another good year. Come on. Oysters? Softshell crabs?"

"Well. . . ."

"Chicken. Nickel just loves chicken." Leroy smiled.

"All right." She resigned herself to our perversity.

The waitress came and Louise ordered, adding cole slaw, fries, and some rolls.

Mother returned. "All right, kid, your turn. Go back to the car and get your clothes out of the trunk."

How glad I was to peel off my bathing suit, which I hated, dry off, and pull a clean T-shirt over my head, put on shorts, wipe my feet, and slip my feet into cotton socks and my PF Flyers, which weren't as bright as Leroy's.

The food, spilling over paper plates, covered the trestle table when I returned. Crabhouses— outdoor beach shacks—usually used paper plates and disposable utensils to save time for the help. Saved money, too. The only thing they had to wash were pots and pans, and they would scrub down on the wooden tables with a heavy scrapper and boiling water.

Mother and Louise were pulling apart their softshell crabs: all those legs, somehow it seemed obscene. Those dead little eyes on their stalks gave me the creeps but I wasn't about to let Leroy know.

When we were finished, the owner, a young handsome man, came by, "How was it, folks?"

"Delicious." Louise smiled up.

His hair was wavy, bleached in the sun, and his tanned face contrasted with his white teeth.

Mother opined, "Those were the best softshell crabs I ever ate."

He lingered, flirting with Mother—men always did that. Then he left.

"How come men always talk to you?" Leroy carefully folded his napkin, unaware that such a question might hurt Louise's feelings.

"Oh, I pretend I'm interested in everything

they say. That's the secret to men." She took Leroy's plate and napkin. "Actually, that's the secret to people. Listen."

"I'm not listening to Nickel. She gets me in trouble." He looked earnestly from Mother to Louise. "She told me if I took my pants off a big bird would swoop down and grab my pecker."

"Nickel?" Mother reached for my plate, too.

"It would."

"Why?" Louise also tidied up.

"Because the bird would think Leroy's part was a juicy worm."

Louise frowned, "I don't know what gets into your head but you shouldn't talk like that. It's not proper."

"Yes, Ma'am."

Leroy gloated.

Mother stood up but she hadn't yet folded up our plates, and I snatched one of the big claws off the softshell crab carcass. With stealth I moved it up to Leroy's eye.

"Plucked a dead man's eye right out of his head."

Leroy screamed, knocked my hand up so the claw sailed upward then landed in the crushed shells of the parking lot. "Did not."

"Mmm, yummy."

"You leave me alone."

The two sisters, accustomed to children bouncing from tears to laughter to rage, were unfazed, and the exchange instantly died down when they stared at us.

Since neither Mother nor Louise had seen the claw fall I picked it up when Leroy headed back to the car. I wiped it off, wrapped it in a napkin that had been sitting on another table, and secreted it in my shorts pocket.

Back in the car, Louise slid onto the folded towel and turned on the car. "Juts, let's go back just for a minute and see if our castle is still standing."

"Sure. As long as we're home by seven."

"Unless there's an accident, we should be." Louise backed out.

Small clapboard houses, most of them set back off the road, decreased in number as we headed back to the Point. Painted shutters adorned each building, testimony to the storms that would roar off the Bay.

People had begun to leave the beach as the afternoon light lengthened.

"Leroy, before we drive home I want you to change out of those trunks, wash off, and put your shorts on. All right?"

"Yes, Ma'am. After we come back from the sand castle."

The castle stood, not even a pennant removed.

"How about that?" Mother touched Leroy's hand.

"This is our best one."

"You say that every year." Mother slipped her arm through Louise's.

"Funny. I wonder how many sand castles

we've built since we were kids? It goes so fast, Juts, so fast."

"I know."

"Scares me."

"Me, too."

They stood there as Leroy knelt down to study the drawbridge.

"You can raise and lower it but you have to be careful. Have to use your hand because I didn't build a winch," Mother told him.

I knelt down beside him as he slid his fingernails under the top of the drawbridge, which he then lowered.

Inside the castle, a small crab had dug in the sand. We hadn't noticed but then she wasn't advertising her presence. The lowered drawbridge roused her and she dashed sideways across it and right over Leroy's hand. He screamed and fell back and the small crab fell back with him darting into the wide leg of his bathing trunks.

"Oww," Leroy hollered, tears in his eyes.

I paid him no mind figuring he was being a big baby because he had fallen. How can he hurt himself in the sand?

Then he really started to scream.

Mother and Louise came over to lift him up but he grabbed his trunks.

Mother knelt down, Leroy, what's wrong?"

"Oww."

Louise, kneeling down now, too, pulled out his waistband. "Julia, the crab's latched onto him."

The two quickly pulled off his trunks. Sure enough, the crab held his part in her claw, probably as upset as Leroy but not about to release her grip.

Mother grabbed the crab from behind, thumb on belly, forefinger on top of her yellowish shell with its blue edges. "Sis, see if you can pry open the claw."

Louise reached for the claw but the crab waved its other one menacingly. "Nickel, grab a pennant off the sandcastle. Now!"

I did, handing her the popsicle stick with the colored paper on the end. She put it in front of the crab, who grabbed it.

"You want me to do it and you hold the crab?" Mother asked Louise.

"No, I think I can do it."

Leroy cried and sobbed so hard he couldn't even scream anymore.

Louise put her fingers on both sides of the claw. "Damn. Nickel get another pennant."

I did.

Perspiration gleamed on her forehead.

"Honey, be ready to put the popsicle stick into the claw the minute she gets it off," Mother commanded.

Finally, Louise pried open the claw and before the crab could pinch her I stuck the popsicle stick into the claw. The little crustacean snapped at the stick just as Mother threw her on the sand, where she ran sideways with two popsicle sticks.

It would have been funny if Leroy hadn't been in so much pain.

"Honey, honey, move your hands." Louise had gently tried to move his hand away from his penis the second the crab had been pulled off.

"No."

"Leroy, do as you're told." Louise's voice sharpened. "This isn't something to fool around with."

He removed his hands, doubled up now.

Mother said, "Thank God she didn't cut through him, but she took a slice."

"He'll swell up and that's going to hurt, too. Juts, let's carry him back to the car and we'll find some ice."

"I can walk," he cried, but he could hardly stand when they got him up. "Give me my trunks."

"All right. All right." Louise handed him his trunks and he fell over putting one leg in.

"I'll run to the shower and wet a towel. We can wipe him off," I volunteered.

"Hurry." Mother leaned down to lift Leroy up.

"I'll walk."

He did, painfully, as Louise held his hand.

I was already at the pump when they drove up. Leroy was helped out of the car by Mother. She wiped off his part, then rewet the towel, wiping the sand off him very quickly.

Back in the car in no time, Louise found a filling station with an ice machine sitting outside. She bought a bag of ice, put it in her bucket, and raced back to the car.

"Nickel, get a small towel out of the trunk."

I did, and the sisters put the towel under him, then wrapped ice cubes in another towel I handed them.

"You have to hold this on you even if the cold sort of makes you throb after a while," Louise ordered him. "When the ice melts have Nickel put more in the towel. Do like I tell you and you'll be all right."

He nodded as Mother handed him the towel. "Hold it right over where the crab grabbed you."

Mother checked her watch as they drove away. "We won't get back in time to take him to the doctor."

"I hope he doesn't need one but if it doesn't look good I'll ask Doc Ferguson to come over. You don't want to take chances with something like that."

"Those claws are sharp. That damned little crab could have nipped a ball right off if she'd hit him right," Mother stated offhandedly.

"Really?" The lurid image compelled me.

"Are you all right, Leroy?" Mother ignored me.

"It hurts."

"It's going to hurt for a while." Mother turned to Louise. "We could give him half an aspirin."

"Mmm, not yet. I don't like giving stuff like that to kids."

"We could give him children's aspirin."

"I'd have to go all the way into Leonardtown and that would cost us an hour." Louise's hands gripped the steering wheel at ten o'clock and four o'clock. "It's more important to get home."

"You're right." Mother uttered the magic words. A bit later she said—voice low but I was straining to listen—"I don't think any veins are cut. There's some blood but I don't think a vein was hit. There'd be more blood."

"Let's hope."

"They get crooked after an injury."

"I know. Marie said after Bill broke his pelvis, his part never straightened out. Now why is that? Why would breaking his pelvis affect his part?" Louise was recalling a conversation with one of her pals.

Mother stared out the window; there was a beautiful small white church in the distance. "I don't know. We think men are uncomplicated, that part of them, but I'm not so sure. Seems to be a lot of problems in that area. Bill's not the only one. Remember when Tommy Lavery passed out then came to and threw up? We thought he had an appendicitis attack but it was one of those tubes from his testicle that got twisted although the pain was in his guts." Mother shook her head. "Must have been just awful."

I pretended not to listen. The ice was melting so I wrung the towel out into the ice bucket, plucked out more cubes, wrapped them up, and handed it to Leroy.

"Usually you can see if something's wrong down there," Louise replied. "But sometimes you can't. Course, when we have female troubles you can't see a thing."

"You and I have been very lucky on that front," Mother changed the subject. "Remember when we were teenagers and everything was happening? I mean, you'd wake up to a different body? All of a sudden breasts appeared."

Louise smiled. "God, I wouldn't go back and do that over for all the tea in China."

"But did you ever think what it's like for boys? No control. Their part stands up at the darnedest times. How embarrassing."

"Sure made us all laugh, though, didn't it?"

"I'm not one hundred percent sure they ever really get it under control. Reach a certain age and it doesn't work right or it stands up but then dies on you."

Louise raised an eyebrow. "Chessy," she used Dad's name, "having problems?"

"No. But you hear about it, you know?"

"Oh."

They launched into a discussion of their girl-friends and their husbands. I tuned out. Leroy fell asleep.

Silence in the back alerted Mother. She turned around.

"He's asleep."

"I can see that." She half rose, got on her knees, and leaned over the front seat. "Hold the ice on him for awhile. When it's all melted you can stop. That ought to help."

"I'm not touching him."

"Nickel."

Just the way she said my name made me grimace. I reached over because his hand had slipped, repositioned the small towel, and held it while I plotted some future, great revenge.

The ice seemed to melt at a glacial rate. My left arm was tired from holding the towel straight and I hated the procedure. Every now and then Mother would turn around.

"It's almost melted," I lied.

"Wait until it's all gone."

I must have pushed down a little harder than necessary because he woke with a whimper. I pulled my hand away as though it was on fire.

"Hey!" He was as horrified as I was.

"Mother made me do it," I quickly proclaimed.

Mother whirled around, "Yes, I did. Leroy," a long pause followed, "we want to make sure you're all right. That everything works. You'll thank us when you're married."

"I'm never getting married." He put his hand over the towel.

"Me neither." I folded my arms over my chest.

"Does it still hurt?" Louise asked, never taking her eyes off the road.

"It's cold."

"Does it throb?" Louise prodded.

"I don't know."

"How can you not know?" I giggled.

"Cause I can't feel anything. It's too cold. The cold hurts."

"Well, take the towel off for a while and if it swells up or starts to really throb then put ice back on." Mother then addressed me. "See that he does, Nick."

"Mom, I don't want to. . . ." I didn't finish.

96

"I can do it. I'm not going to fall asleep." He leaned toward me and whispered. "You touch my pecker and you die."

"I'll kill you first. I don't want to touch that silly worm and besides, there was a towel on it. I never really touched you, Leroy."

"You say."

I readied to hit him, then remembered he was incapacitated, sort of, so I folded my arms back over my chest and stared out the window.

"Look, you two, this is going to be a long ride. I don't want to hear a peep." Louise shook her head as she did when we irritated her.

The ice finally did melt and Leroy removed his towel, looked down. He put the towel in the bucket while covering himself.

Mother noticed the movement, "Well?"

"I'm okay."

"Is it swollen?" She continued her line of questioning.

"No."

"Leroy, how does it look?" Louise had had enough.

"It's cut a little but it's not swollen."

"Is it discolored?" Louise wanted to know.

"Uh," he was at a loss.

"Wheezie, he had the ice on it so it's probably a little blue.

Mother's reply to her sister made Leroy look at his part. "Color's coming back."

"Some pain might come back with it," Mother said, then joked, "Honey, we want that part to work. My sister can't wait to be a great-grandmother."

Because Louise married at sixteen, Ginny born a year after, and Ginny married at sixteen, chances were strong that Louise might live long enough to see great-great grandchildren if they kept marrying so young.

Mother, on the other hand, waited until her midtwenties to marry, being in no hurry to be tied down. Her endless sociability gave Louise the vapors and the platinum wedding ring on her finger never produced the staidness that Louise thought would follow. If anything, Mother threw herself into even more activities and when I appeared she threw me into them, too. I was probably the only child in the state of Maryland happy to go to bed at night. I needed the rest.

"I'm not getting married." Leroy repeated, with more vehemence.

"We'll see." Louise used her singsong voice, which we both hated.

"I'm not! I don't want children. I want my mother!" His face shone crimson.

Mother told him soothingly, "We all do, honey, we all do."

"The Lord giveth and the Lord taketh away," Louise said.

"Why? Why, Wheezie?" He shouted. "Why did He take Mama when there are old people to take? Everything God makes dies."

Frightened from his outburst and his sorrow, I wedged myself up against the door.

"Wheeze, pull over," Mother ordered.

A stunned expression crossed Louise's pretty features. She pulled over. Mother got out and opened the door. Had I not been hanging onto the door handle I would have plopped onto the side of the road.

"Nickel, come up with me," Louise ordered softly.

"Yes, Ma'am."

Mother patted my shoulder as I lurched out then slid onto the front seat and closed the door. She closed the back door, moving next to Leroy, and put her arms around him. He buried his face in her soft bosom and sobbed his heart out.

Louise pulled back onto the road. When I looked around Mother was crying, too, and that made me cry—that and everything.

Louise, tears in her eyes, gently said, "Nickel, sometimes God seems cruel. We can't understand it. You have to believe and you have to be strong. Only the strong survive."

"Yes, Ma'am."

Louise swallowed hard and reached for my left hand with her right. She gave it a hard squeeze, regaining her composure.

When I next looked around Leroy had fallen asleep on Mother's breasts, her blouse soaked by his tears. She held the towel over his part but it didn't have ice in it. She smiled at me but put her finger to her lips. I smiled back.

I stayed awake, which I usually did in the car because I lived in fear that I'd miss something. I loved to look at fields full of cattle and see if I could count them before they were out of sight. Houses, churches, stores, road signs, colors, big trees, it all fascinated me. Sometimes I could even identify birds in flight or see a big Red-tailed Hawk perched in a tree waiting for supper. I didn't say a word until Louise dropped us off at our house and Leroy woke up.

Mother kissed him, pulled his pants up as he woke. "You'll be okay."

He hugged her.

"Leroy, come on up here with me," Louise said.

He opened the car door and walked around but he walked funny, keeping his legs apart. I kissed him, too.

As we walked toward the back door I remembered the crab claw in my pocket so as Mother moved ahead—she always walked so fast—I dumped out the claw.

Dad came into the kitchen when he heard the back door open. He gave Mother a big kiss and one to me, too. Dad was a hugger and kisser but he especially liked kissing Mother.

"How was your day?"

"Chessy, I don't even know where to start."

I did. "Daddy, a crab bit Leroy's pecker!"

Dad's beautiful blue eyes widened. He turned to Mother. "I hope it was a female crab."

* * *

As I write this I am fourteen years older than Mother and Dad were back then. They're all gone. Louise made it to one hundred if you believed her birthday. Chances were she had tipped over the century mark.

Leroy and I kept our promise. Neither of us did marry. He became a marine just like his father. He was killed in Vietnam.

Louise kept the flag the marines gave her at the funeral. I have it now, folded in a triangle, on my bookshelf. I put a plastic crab on it.